For my grandmother and my mother

V. d'Heur

For my mother, who was never afraid of anything,

especially not the way ahead

L. Bourguignon

MYRIAD BOOKS LIMITED
35 Bishopsthorpe Road, London SE26 4PA

First published in 2004 by
MIJADE PUBLICATIONS
16-18, rue de l'Ouvrage
5000 Namur-Belgium

© Laurence Bourguignon and Valérie d'Heur, 2004

Translation: Lisa Pritchard

Laurence Bourguignon and Valérie d'Heur have
asserted their right to be identified as the author
and illustrator of this work in accordance with the
Copyright, Designs and Patents Act, 1988.

ISBN 1 84746 038 0

Printed in China

Old Elephant

Laurence Bourguignon

Valérie d'Heur

MYRIAD BOOKS LIMITED

Tiny Mouse and Old Elephant
lived under the same tree.

Tiny Mouse slept in a hole in the roots, and
Old Elephant leaned against the tree-trunk.

Tiny Mouse was clever. She made a cord
so that Old Elephant wouldn't lose his glasses.

That was a good idea, because Old Elephant's
eyesight was not very good any more.

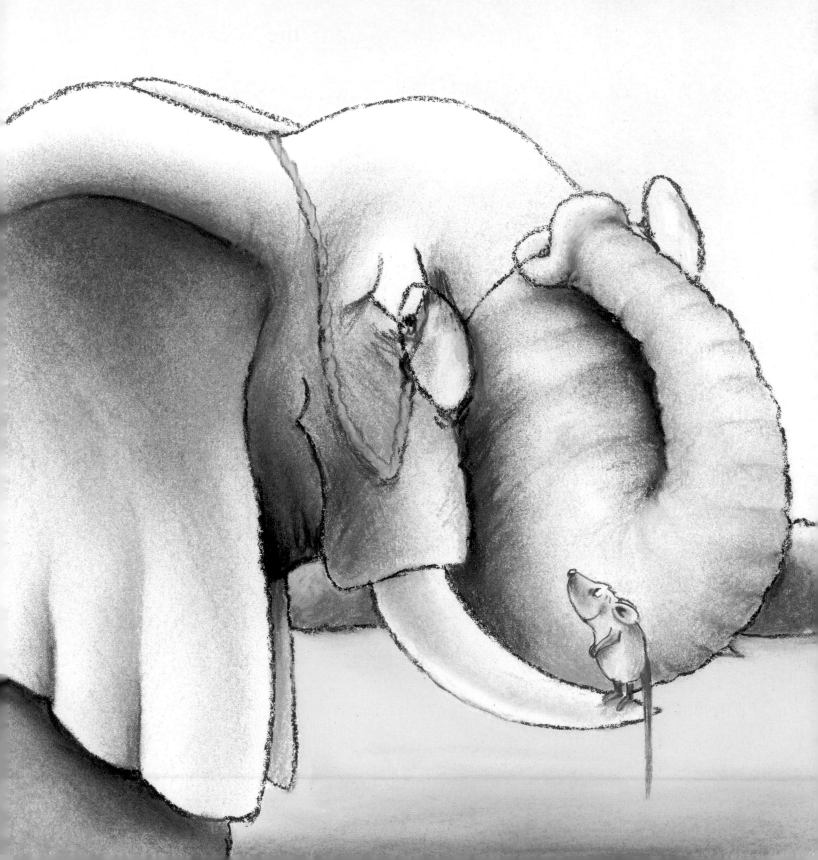

Old Elephant was strong. He took care of Tiny Mouse when she was very young. He often took her for a walk to faraway places that her little legs would never have carried her.

They went to the mountain…

…and to the big lake.

Tiny Mouse was a little ray of sunshine in Old Elephant's life. He was often very tired. He had seen so much!

Sometimes he closed his eyes and remembered his old friends Bambam and Aragorn. They had gone to the Valley of the Elephants a long time ago.

Was it time for Old Elephant to follow them?

One evening, after his bath, he set off on a different track.

"Where are we going, Old Elephant?" asked Tiny Mouse.

"You'll see," said Old Elephant.

When they got to the forest, the plants had grown over the path, but the ground was hard as if giant animals had been there before them.

"Do you remember when I told you about the place that elephants go to when they are old and sick?"

"I remember," said Tiny Mouse.

"It's over there!" said Old Elephant. The path had led them to the edge of the jungle. They stood at the top of a very deep ravine.

On the other side there was a beautiful forest that stretched as far as the eye could see.

"That's where my parents went, and my brothers, and all my friends. Soon I'll go there too. It won't be sad. Elephants are happy over there."

Tiny Mouse felt her heart beat faster. Old Elephant had already talked about this but she didn't want to have to think about it.

Suddenly, Old Elephant saw something. He called out.

"What's wrong, Old Elephant?" cried Tiny Mouse. Then she saw what he was looking at: he would never get to the other side.

Old Elephant was thinking. He was too heavy and too clumsy to fix the bridge. But Tiny Mouse would be able to do it.

Her little voice interrupted his thoughts: "If I mend the knots and you go across, will you come back, Old Elephant?"

He hardly paused before he answered, "No. You don't come back from there."

"But I don't want you to go!" cried Tiny Mouse. "I want you to stay with me forever."

Old Elephant nodded. Without saying a word he turned round and they went back to their tree.

Life carried on as before. Old Elephant
pretended there was nothing wrong and
so did Tiny Mouse.

But she often thought about it,
and it made her afraid.

Time passed… Tiny Mouse was bigger now.
She was the one who led the way and found
the fruit for their meals. Even with his glasses on
Old Elephant couldn't see much. He was more
and more forgetful…

… and he was going deaf.
Tiny Mouse had to shout
when she talked to him.

They still laughed and had fun
like before. But Old Elephant
was careful not to laugh too
much because these days it
made him cough.

Then he started to cough even when he hadn't been laughing.
Tiny Mouse made him a blanket to keep him warm
during the cold nights.

But Old Elephant coughed
and coughed as he leaned
against the trunk.

He didn't eat the fruit that Tiny
Mouse brought him, even his
favourite bananas.

"I'm not hungry," he said every time, and closed his eyes.

Now Tiny Mouse understood that he was very ill. She remembered what Old Elephant had told her.

One day when he was too old or too ill, he would have to go away.

But now she was not so little, and she wasn't as frightened as before. She was sad, of course, at the thought of seeing her friend leave.

She knew he would be happy over there, so she worked as fast and as carefully as she could. The bridge would have to be strong to carry the weight of Old Elephant.

Old Elephant was waiting for her under their tree.

She climbed up his leg, just as she always did, and whispered into his ear.

Old Elephant didn't look surprised.

He winked at her and said, "I knew I could count on you."

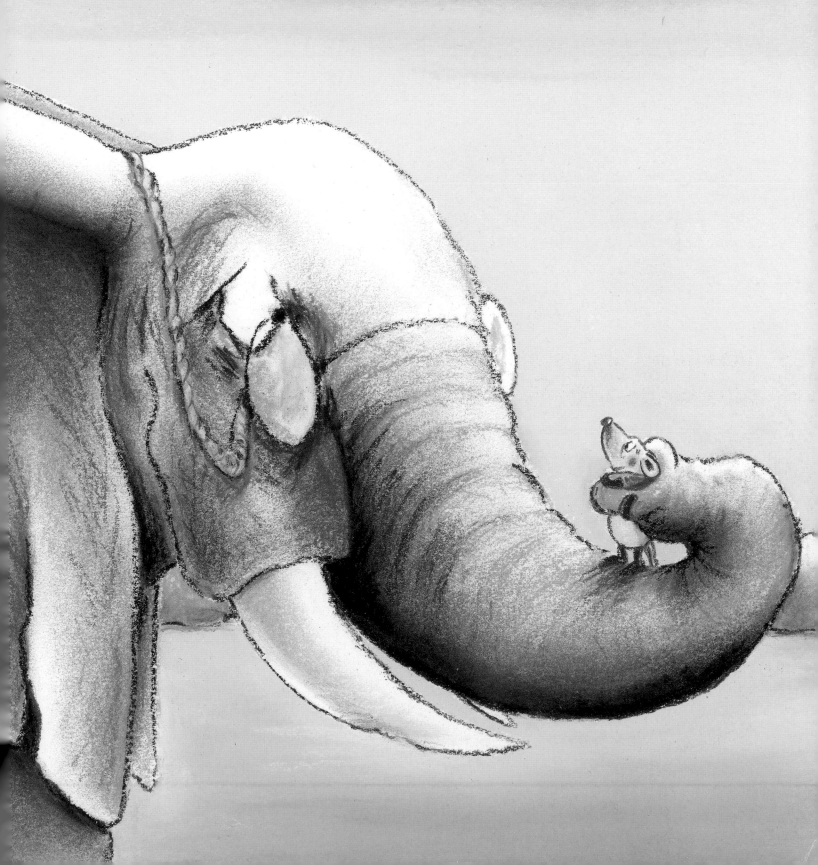

He stepped firmly out onto the bridge.

"Don't be afraid," cried Tiny Mouse. "It's safe now."

Old Elephant stopped and turned his head. "I'm not afraid,"
he said. "Everything will be all right, I know."

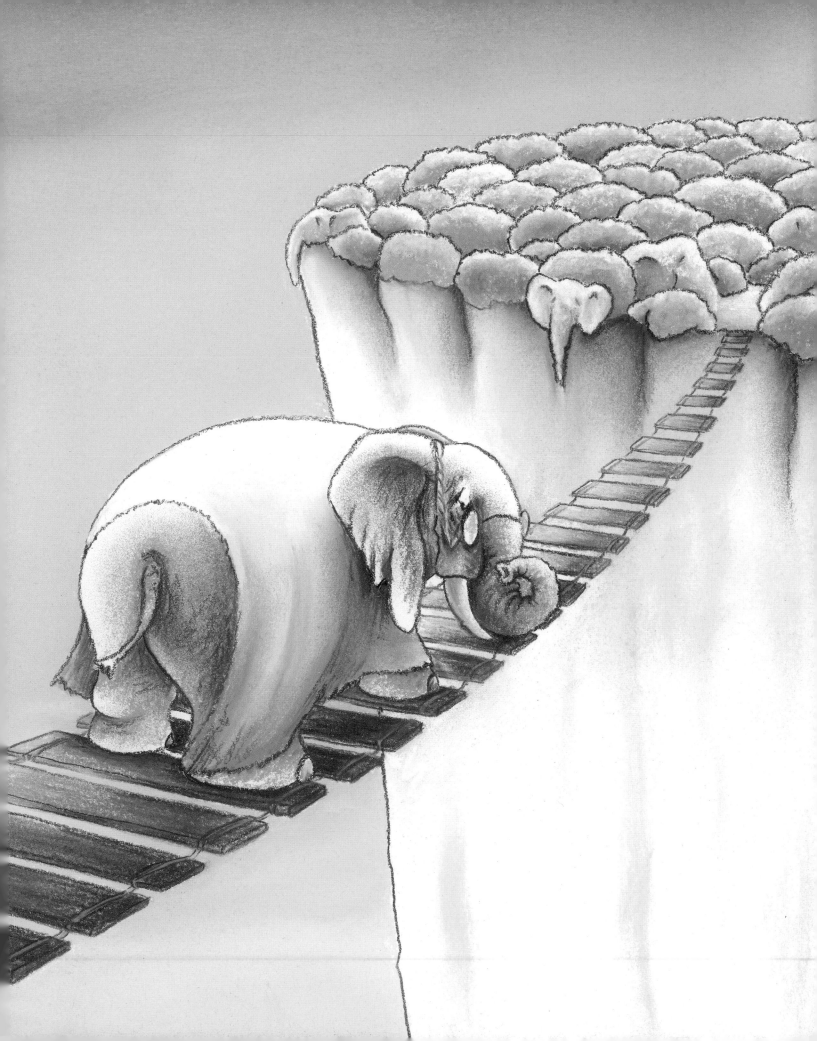

"Yes, everything will be all right,"
murmured Tiny Mouse to herself.
And she gave a little smile.

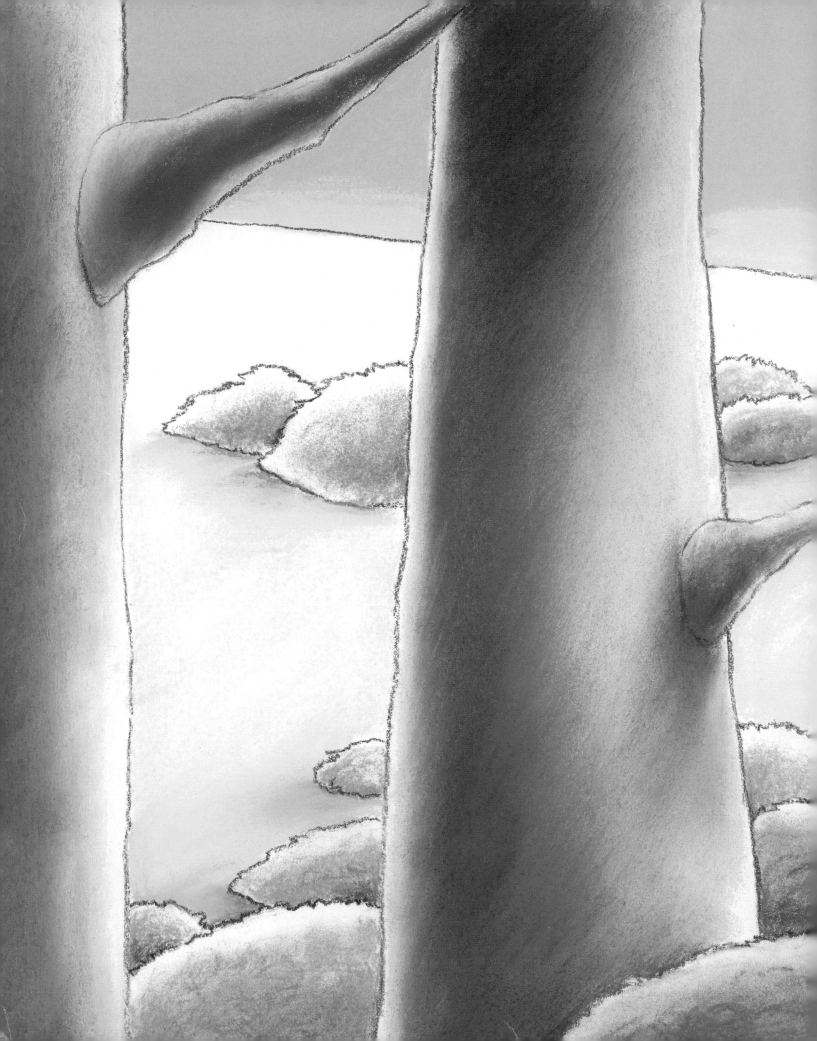